W9-AKB-345

DATE DUE

MR 28	MY 1'89	JUL 19 '90	
AP22'86	MY 13'89	APR 18 15	
SE 8'86	AG 11'89	AG 11 08	
OC22'86	OC17'89	Y 07 5	
AP 2'87	NO14 89		
AP20'87	DE 5 89		
MY31'88	JE 6'90	AP 20 17	
JE09'88	JY10'90		
JY14'88	UY 21'90		
DE13 88	JY25'90		
JA19'89	AP 8'91		
MR24'89	AG15'92		

E
Mot
Mother Goose
Mary had a little lamb
and other favorites

This book belongs to

_____

MOTHER GOOSE'S NURSERY RHYMES

MARY HAD A LITTLE LAMB
AND OTHER FAVORITES

ILLUSTRATED BY
ALLEN ATKINSON

AN ARIEL BOOK

BANTAM BOOKS
TORONTO · NEW YORK · LONDON · SYDNEY · AUCKLAND

MARY HAD A LITTLE LAMB AND OTHER FAVORITES
A Bantam Book
April 1985

Art Direction: Armand Eisen and Tom Durwood

All rights reserved.
Copyright © 1985 by The Tempest Company.
This book may not be reproduced in whole or in part, by
mimeograph or any other means, without permission.
For information address: Bantam Books, Inc.

ISBN 0-553-15319-6

Published simultaneously in the United States and Canada

Bantam Books are published by Bantam Books, Inc. Its trademark,
consisting of the words "Bantam Books" and the portrayal of a rooster, is
Registered in U.S. Patent and Trademark Office and in other countries.
Marca Registrada. Bantam Books, Inc., 666 Fifth Avenue, New York,
New York 10103.

Printing and binding by
Printer, industria gráfica S.A.   Provenza, 388   Barcelona
Depósito legal B. 332-1985
PRINTED IN SPAIN
0 9 8 7 6 5 4 3 2 1

"No, no, my melodies will never die,
While nurses sing or babies cry."
—Mother Goose

MARY HAD A little lamb,
Its fleece was white as snow;
And everywhere that Mary went
The lamb was sure to go.

MOTHER GOOSE'S NURSERY RHYMES

It followed her to school one day,
That was against the rule;
It made the children laugh and play,
To see a lamb in school.

And so the teacher turned it out,
But still it lingered near,
And waited patiently about
Till Mary did appear.

Why does the lamb love Mary so?
The eager children cry.
Why, Mary loves the lamb, you know,
The teacher did reply.

MARY HAD a pretty bird,
Feathers bright and yellow,
Slender legs, upon my word,
He was a pretty fellow.

The sweetest notes he always sang,
Which much delighted Mary;
And near the cage she'd ever sit,
To hear her own canary.

HICKORY, dickory, dock!
The mouse ran up the clock.
The clock struck one,
The mouse ran down.
Hickory, dickory, dock!

As I was going to St. Ives,
I met a man with seven wives,
Each wife had seven sacks,
Each sack had seven cats,
Each cat had seven kits.
Kits, cats, sacks, and wives,
How many were going to St. Ives?

RIDE A COCK-HORSE to Banbury Cross,
To see a fine lady upon a white horse;
Rings on her fingers and bells on her toes,
And she shall have music wherever she goes.

MOTHER GOOSE'S NURSERY RHYMES

A DILLER, a dollar
A ten o'clock scholar,
What makes you come so soon?
You used to come at ten o'clock,
And now you come at noon.

MOTHER GOOSE'S NURSERY RHYMES

HUSH, LITTLE BABY, don't say a word,
Papa's going to buy you a mockingbird.

MOTHER GOOSE'S NURSERY RHYMES

If the mockingbird won't sing,
Papa's going to buy you a diamond ring.

If the diamond ring turns brass,
Papa's going to buy you a looking glass.

MOTHER GOOSE'S NURSERY RHYMES

If the looking glass gets broke,
Papa's going to buy you a billy goat.

If the billy goat runs away,
Papa's going to buy you another today.

MOTHER GOOSE'S NURSERY RHYMES

BAA, BAA, black sheep,
Have you any wool?
Yes sir, yes sir,
Three bags full:
One for my master,
One for my dame,
One for the little boy
Who lives down the lane.

I HAD A little nut tree,
Nothing would it bear
But a silver nutmeg
And a golden pear.
The king of Spain's daughter
Came to visit me,
And all for the sake
Of my little nut tree.

RAIN, RAIN, go away,
Come again another day.

OLD FATHER Long-Legs
Can't say his prayers;
Take him by the left leg,
And throw him down the stairs.
And when he's at the bottom,
Before he long has lain,
Take him by the right leg,
And throw him up again.

FOUR AND twenty tailors
Went to kill a snail;
The best man among them
Dared not touch her tail.
She put out her horns
Like a little Kyloe cow;
Run, tailors, run,
Or she'll kill you all e'en now.

MOTHER GOOSE'S NURSERY RHYMES

THIRTY DAYS hath September,
April, June, and November;
All the rest have thirty-one,
Excepting February alone,
And that has twenty-eight days clear
And twenty-nine in each leap year.

MOTHER GOOSE'S NURSERY RHYMES

PUNCH AND JUDY
Fought for a pie,
Punch gave Judy
A sad blow in the eye.

Says Punch to Judy,
Will you have more?
Says Judy to Punch,
My eye is sore.

MOTHER GOOSE'S NURSERY RHYMES

THREE WISE MEN of Gotham,
They went to sea in a bowl.
And if the bowl had been stronger,
My song had been longer.

Peter White will ne'er go right;
Would you know the reason why?
He follows his nose wherever he goes,
And that stands all awry.

ROSES ARE RED, violets are blue,
Honey is sweet, and so are you.
Thou art my love and I am thine;
I drew thee to my Valentine.
The lot was cast and then I drew,
And fortune said it should be you.

MOTHER GOOSE'S NURSERY RHYMES

Something old,

something new,

Something borrowed,

something blue,

And a penny in her shoe.

MISTRESS MARY, quite contrary,
How does your garden grow?
With silver bells and cockleshells
And pretty maids all in a row.

GOLDEN SLUMBERS kiss your eyes,
Smiles awake you when you rise.
Sleep pretty darling, do not cry,
And I will sing you a lullaby:
Rock them, rock them, lullaby.

Care is heavy, therefore sleep you;
You are care, and care must keep you.
Sleep, pretty darling, do not cry,
And I will sing you a lullaby:
Rock them, rock them, lullaby.

MOTHER GOOSE'S NURSERY RHYMES

ABOUT THE ILLUSTRATOR

Allen Atkinson is one of America's most beloved illustrators, whose works include *The Tale of Peter Rabbit* and other tales by Beatrix Potter, *The Velveteen Rabbit,* and *Mother Goose's Nursery Rhymes,* among others. Mr. Atkinson lives in rural Connecticut, where he was born and raised. His favorite subjects for his paintings are the well-known children's stories which he read as a child. In addition to book illustrations he enjoys creating toys for children.

Allen Atkinson has designed four charming stuffed bean-bag toys: Humpty Dumpty, Little Miss Muffet, Simple Simon, and a mouse from Three Blind Mice, all based on his artwork in *Mother Goose's Nursery Rhymes.* For information, write to The Toy Works, Box 48, Middle Falls, N.Y. 12848.